The GREAT EGGSCAPE

By
Susan Glass

Art by
Cornelius Van Wright

STAR BRIGHT BOOKS
NEW YORK

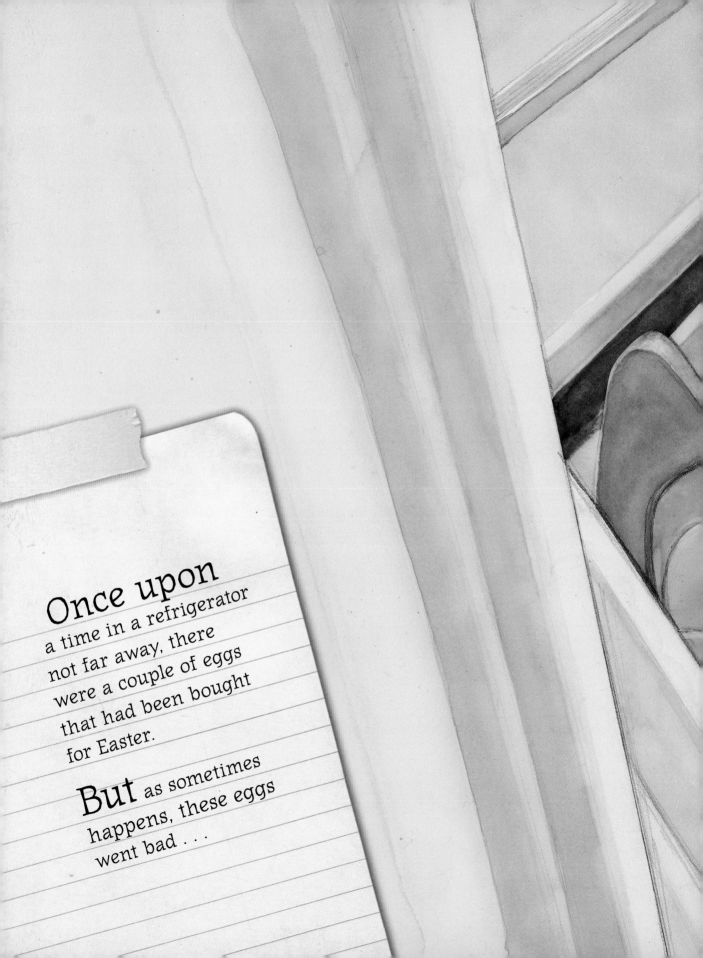

Once upon a time in a refrigerator not far away, there were a couple of eggs that had been bought for Easter.

But as sometimes happens, these eggs went bad . . .

JUST FOR THE FUN OF IT, THEY STARTED TO ROUGH UP THE OTHER INHABITANTS OF THE REFRIGERATOR. FIRST STOP-THE VEGGIE BIN!

THEY MASHED THE POTATOES,

STALKED THE CELERY,

BENNY AND AGGIE ROUGHED UP EVERYONE IN THE FRIDGE. NOBODY KNEW WHAT TO DO ABOUT THEM. BUT THE FOODS KNEW THAT THEY'D HAD ENOUGH!

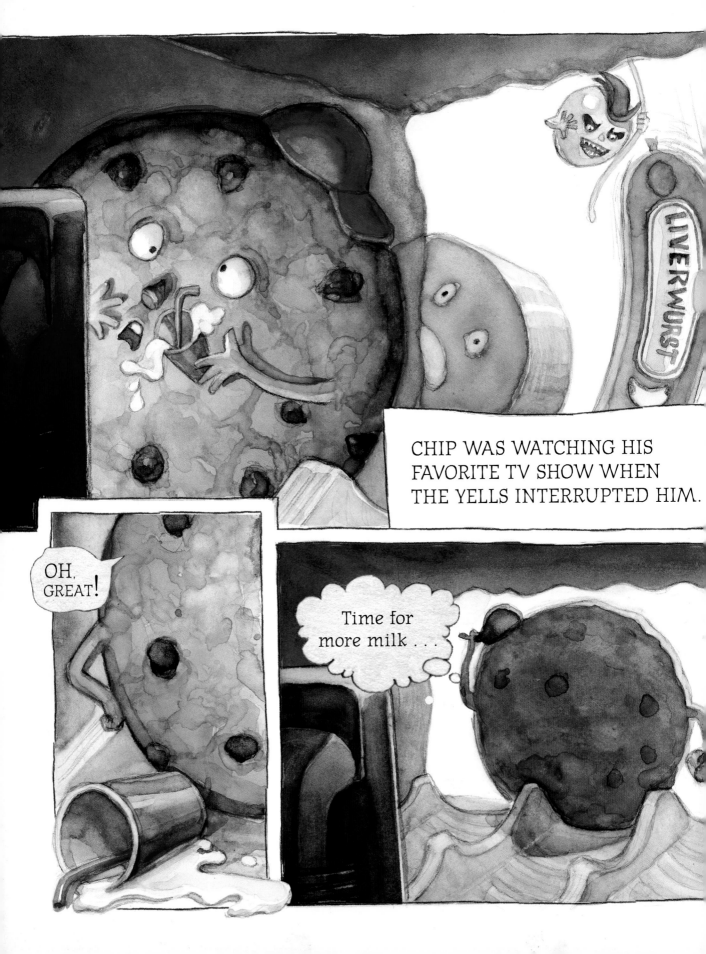

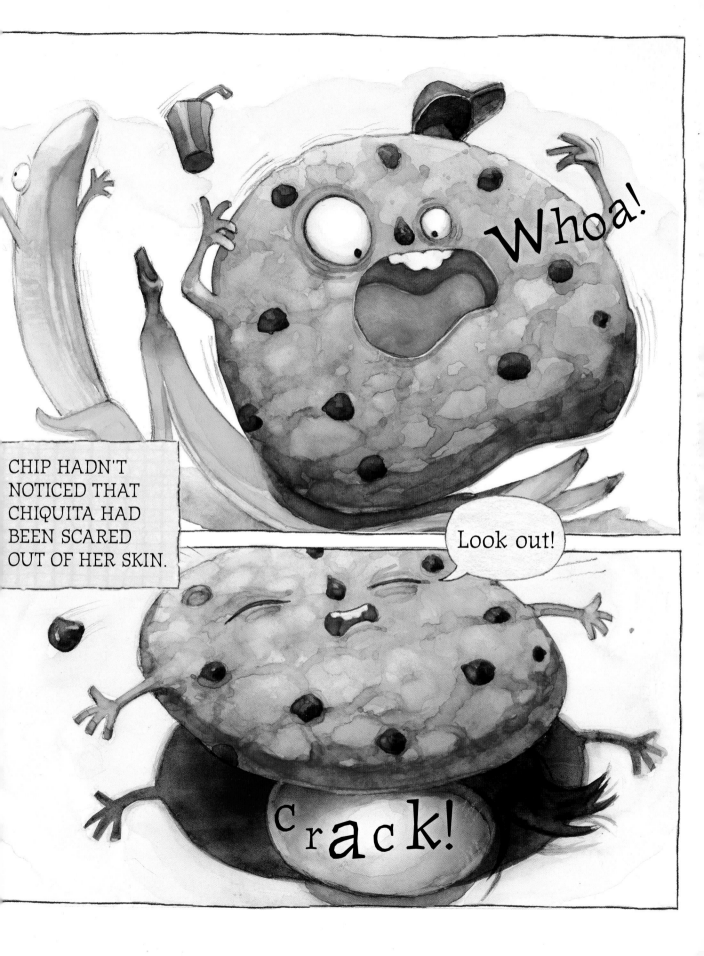

CHIP HADN'T NOTICED THAT CHIQUITA HAD BEEN SCARED OUT OF HER SKIN.

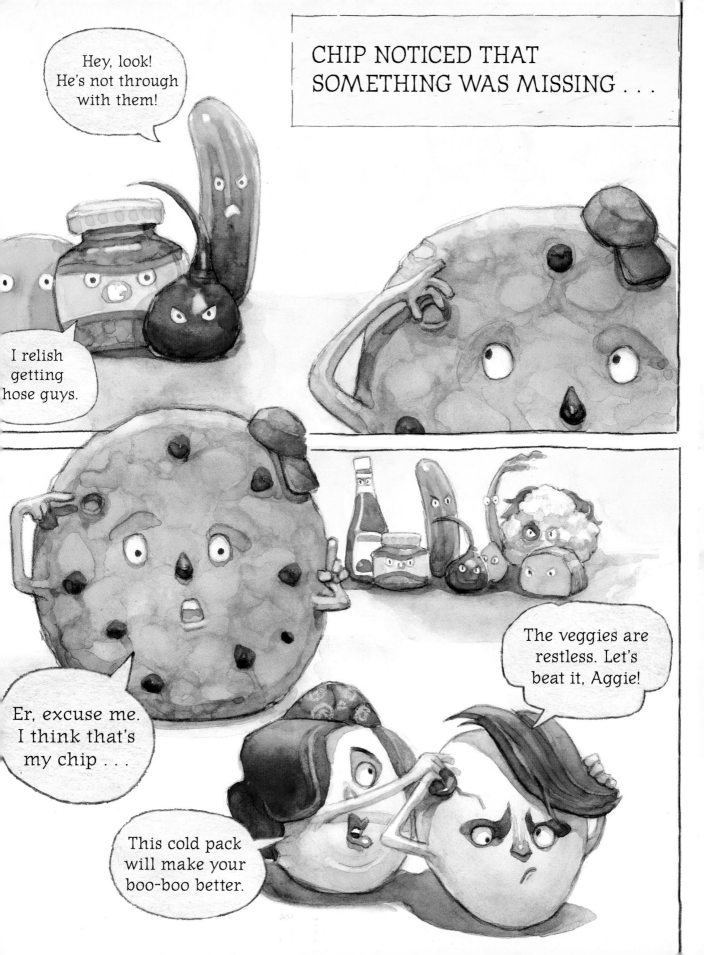

DID AGGIE AND BENNY ESCAPE?

CHIP AND THE GANG CHASED THEM ACROSS THE COUNTER WHILE THE REST WATCHED.

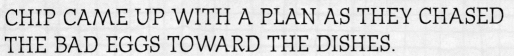

CHIP CAME UP WITH A PLAN AS THEY CHASED
THE BAD EGGS TOWARD THE DISHES.

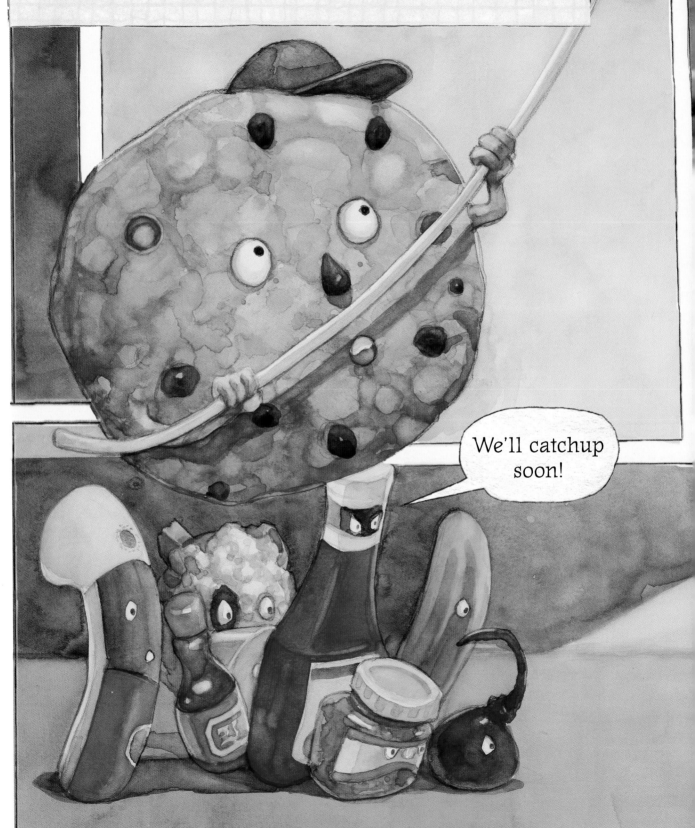

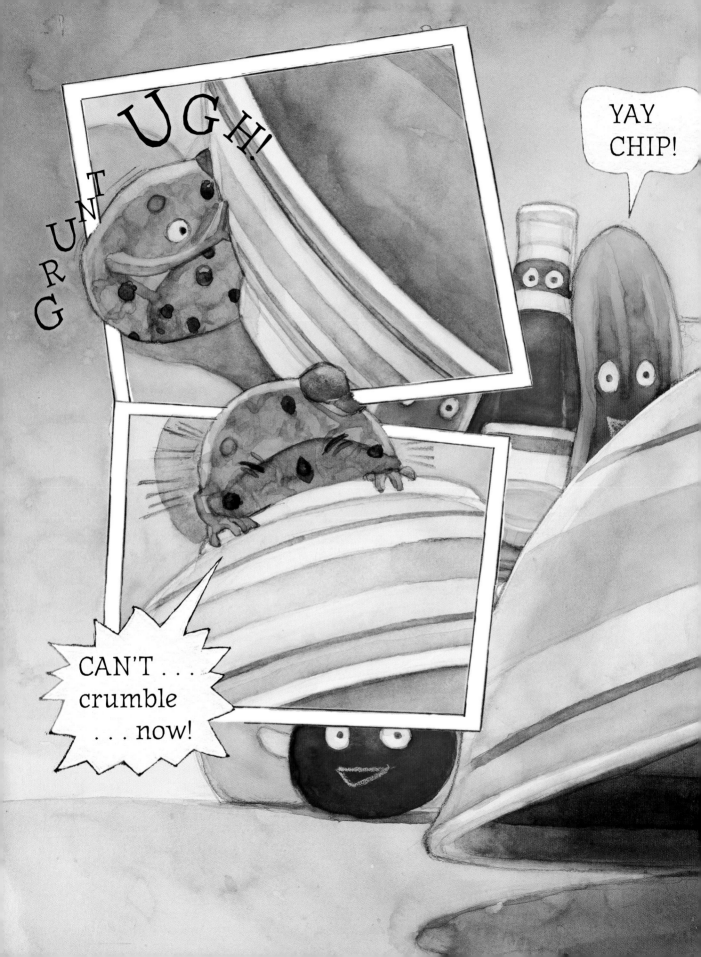

THE BAD EGGS
WERE PUT SAFELY
BEHIND BARS.

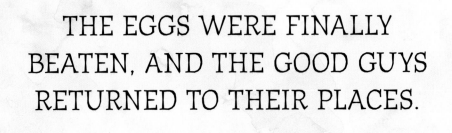

THE EGGS WERE FINALLY
BEATEN, AND THE GOOD GUYS
RETURNED TO THEIR PLACES.

BENNY AND AGGIE WERE
STILL BEHIND BARS WHEN
THEY WERE DISCOVERED
ON EASTER MORNING.
THE BOY STARTED TO EAT
THEM, BUT NOTICED
THAT SOMETHING
WASN'T QUITE RIGHT.

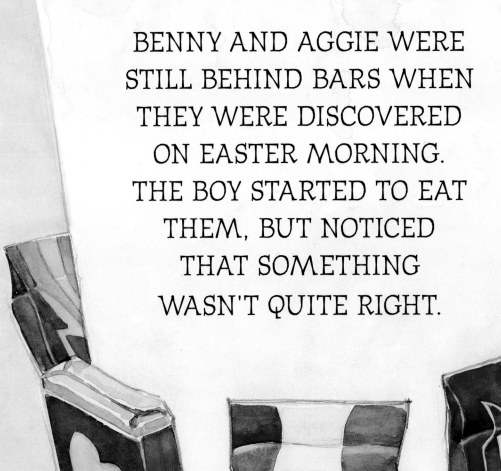

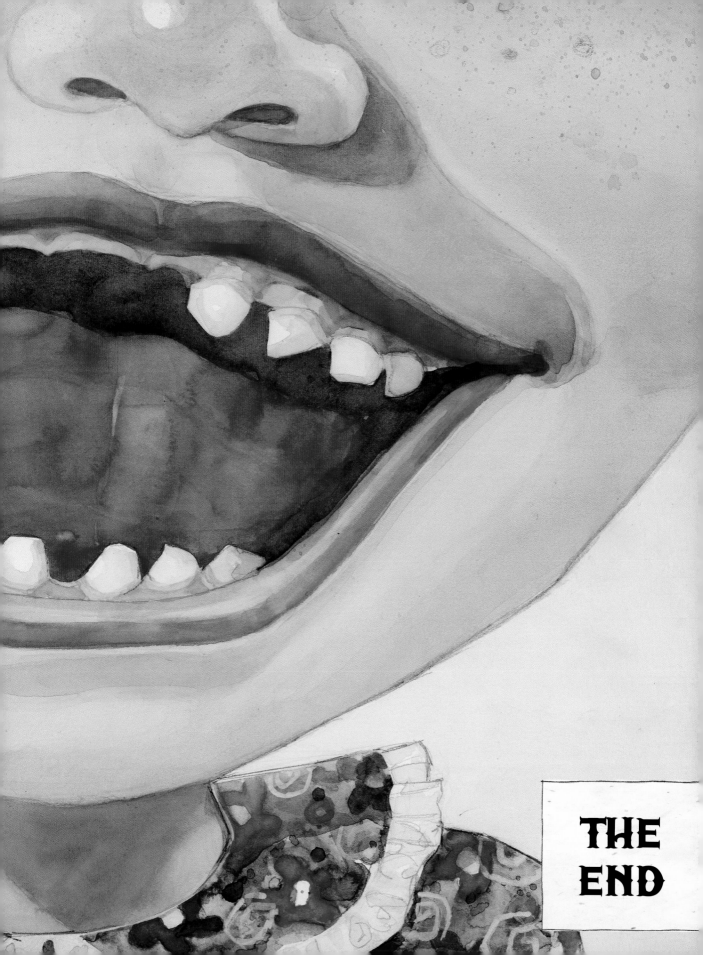

THE
END

Published in the United States of America by Star Bright Books, Inc.,
30-19 48th Avenue, Long Island City, NY 11101.

The name Star Bright Books and the Star Bright Books logo are registered trademarks
of Star Bright Books, Inc. Please visit www.starbrightbooks.com.
For bulk orders, email: orders@starbrightbooks.com.

Hardback ISBN-13: 978-1-59572-261-4
Paperback ISBN-13: 978-1-59572-253-9

Star Bright Books / NY / 00108100
Printed in China (WKT) 9 8 7 6 5 4 3 2 1

Library of Congress Cataloging-in-Publication Data

Glass, Susan.
The great eggscape / by Susan Glass ; illustrations by Cornelius Van Wright.
    p. cm.
Summary: Two rotten eggs wreak havoc on their neighbors, until a hapless cookie becomes an
unlikely hero.
ISBN 978-1-59572-253-9 (pbk. : alk. paper)
[1. Eggs--Fiction. 2. Food--Fiction. 3. Humorous stories.] I. Van Wright, Cornelius, ill. II. Title.
PZ7.G48125Gr 2011
[E]--dc22
                        2009044870